Dedication:

This book is dedicated to my family that encourages me to be the best version of myself. Special thanks to my godfather, Milton Seaton, who always told me that I could get whatever I wanted...you would be proud that I finally listened.

Larry the Lobster has a lot of toys. His friend Daniel the Dinosaur wanted to play with his truck.

"Can I play with your truck", Daniel asked. "No way, leave my stuff alone", Larry replied.

Larry forgot that sharing was caring and he had more than enough to share and care.

Please don't be like Larry. Don't be a selfish shellfish.

Tyler the Turtle and Dennis the Deer were playing at the park. Both of them started throwing sand at each other. Tyler told his parents that Dennis was throwing sand at him. He never mentioned that he was doing the same thing!

Tyler forgot that honesty was the best policy.

Please don't be like Tyler. Don't be a tattling turtle.

Latoya the Lion is always telling stories that are not true. She once told Ashley the Alligator that she used to be an elephant when she was a baby. Latoya forgot that her friends should love her for the person she truly is, and that she didn't need to pretend to be something she was not.

Please don't be like Latoya. Don't be a lying lion.

Robin the Rooster wanted to ask his father a question. His father was talking on the telephone.

"Can I have some cereal", Robin asked. Robin forgot that he was supposed to say excuse me first, and wait until his father gave him permission to speak.

Please don't be like Robin. Don't be a rude rooster.

Latoya the Lion is always telling stories that are not true. She once told Ashley the Alligator that she used to be an elephant when she was a baby. Latoya forgot that her friends should love her for the person she truly is, and that she didn't need to pretend to be something she was not.

Please don't be like Latoya. Don't be a lying lion.

Miss Nice was writing on the board. She was teaching the class how to do some difficult math problems. Everyone was listening, but Donaven the Duck was talking while the teacher was trying to teach the class. Donaven forgot that he was supposed to raise his hand.

Please don't be like Donaven. Don't be a disruptive duck.

Chester the Cheetah was playing a board game with Tom the Tiger. It was Chester's turn to roll the dice. Even though he was only supposed to move five spaces, he moved six. Chester forgot that a true champion wins only if he plays fair.

Please don't be like Chester. Don't be a cheating cheetah.

Kellee the Koala and Robert the Rabbit were playing soccer. Kellee did not want to give Robert a turn, so she kicked him. Kellee forgot that you were not supposed to hurt others.

Please don't be like Kellee. Don't be a kicking koala.

Harry the Hamster and Grampy the Gerbil wanted to have a lemonade stand. Harry wanted to charge $1.00 for each cup, but Grampy only wanted to charge seventy-five cents. They started to argue and Harry hit Grampy. Harry forgot that he was always supposed to keep his hands to himself.

Please don't be like Harry. Don't be a hitting hamster.

Walt the Wolf and Kim the Kangaroo were supposed to go to bed early so they could get enough rest for school the next day. Kim fell fast asleep, but Walt whined about wanting to stay up to watch his favorite movie. Walt forgot that he was supposed to listen to his mother's instructions, without complaining.

Please don't be like Walt. Don't be a whining wolf.

Stella the snake sat next to Ann the Aye Aye. Ann had a beautiful pink glitter pen. Stella loved it! When Ann wasn't looking, Stella took the pen and put it in her backpack. Stella forgot that she was not supposed to take things without permission.

Please don't be like Stella. Don't be a stealing snake.

Miyan the Mockingbird had one chore. Grandma the Goose had asked her to keep her room clean. Miyan forgot that she was supposed to put things back where they belonged when she was finished with them.

Please don't be like Miyan. Don't be a messy mockingbird.

You might be asking yourself:

If I can't be like Larry,
If I can't be like Chester,
If I can't be like Tyler,
If I can't be like Kellee,
If I can't be like Donaven,
If I can't be like Miyan,
If I can't be like Walt,
If I can't be like Latoya,
If I can't be like Robin,
If I can't be like Stella...
Just WHO CAN I BE???!!!

NO RECESS

Larry	Miyan
Chester	Walt
Tyler	Latoya
Kellee	Robin
Donaven	Stella

You can be the best version of yourself!

You can share, tell the truth, use good manners, play fair and be neat and clean. You can also keep your hands and feet to yourself.

JUST BE YOU...BECAUSE YOU CAN CHOOSE TO BE GREAT!

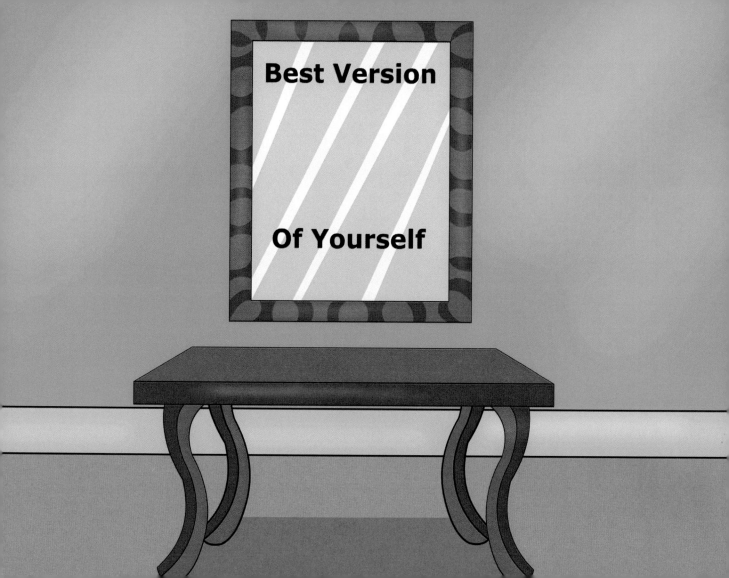

Made in the USA
Columbia, SC
24 February 2023

12937291R00018